DROUGHT

BY
GAIL B. STEWART

CRESTWOOD·HOUSE
New York
Collier Macmillan Canada
Toronto

Maxwell Macmillan International Publishing Group
New York Oxford Singapore Sydney

Library of Congress Cataloging-in-Publication Data
Stewart, Gail, 1949-
  Drought / by Gail B. Stewart. — 1st ed.
      p.   cm. — (Earth alert)
  Includes bibliographical references.
  Summary: Describes droughts around the world, their damaging effects, how people prepare for them, and ways to fight the effects of this type of natural disaster.
  1. Droughts—Juvenile literature. 2. Droughts—United States—Juvenile literature. [1.Droughts.] I. Title.
II. Series.
QC929.D8S83   1990   363.3'492—dc20   90-36293   CIP
ISBN 0-89686-544-4   AC

Photo Credits
Cover: Peter Arnold, Inc. (Bruno Zehnder)
AP—Wide World: 4, 7, 10, 30, 43
Animals Animals/Earth Scenes: (Bruce Davidson) 13; (Brian Milne) 17; (E.R. Degginger) 22, 27; (Bates Littlehales) 33; (Mike Andrews) 39; (Breck P. Kent) 41
Journalism Services: (John E. Bowen) 15
Grant Heilman Photography: (Grant Heilman) 20, 36
Devaney Stock Photos: 25

Macmillan Publishing Company   Collier Macmillan Canada, Inc.
866 Third Avenue   1200 Eglinton Avenue East
New York, NY 10022   Suite 200
                                  Don Mills, Ontario M3C 3N1

CRESTWOOD HOUSE

Produced by Flying Fish Studio Incorporated

Printed in the United States of America

First Edition

10 9 8 7 6 5 4 3 2 1

CONTENTS

A LONG TIME WITHOUT RAIN

Chester Johnson is a 53-year-old farmer from Iowa. He is a good farmer—a careful planner and a hard worker. He has tried to stay current with modern agricultural methods.

"I read a great deal," says Johnson. "I go up to Iowa City a couple of times a year for farming seminars. I like to know what's going on—what's new in machinery and what the scientists have learned about growing things. That helps me be more productive."

But in 1988, Chester Johnson experienced disaster on his farm. What is considered some of the best farmland in the country was baked dry by 100-plus-degree temperatures. Hot winds blew, and almost no rain fell.

None of Chester Johnson's crops grew. Corn and soybeans need lots of moisture to thrive, but no rain came. The few plants that managed to sprout turned brown in the sun.

Johnson lost some of his cattle, too. With no rain, the pasture could not grow green and lush. There weren't many blades of

A drought can be a disaster for farmers, who depend on crops for their livelihood.

grass for the cattle to eat. Sometimes, when an area suffers from lack of rain, farmers in other states help out with extra hay for cattle. But in 1988, almost every farm in the Midwest was as dry as Chester Johnson's.

Some farmers took huge trucks and went north to Canada. They bought hay from farmers there and brought it back for their cattle. But it was not enough. Many grazing animals such as cattle and sheep died because of the hot temperatures and lack of food.

In another part of the world, a farmer from Ethiopia has lost all of his crops, as well as his livestock. In his country, the rains that usually keep his farmland green have been absent. Since 1981, there has been a lack of rain in some parts of Ethiopia.

Since the dry, hot weather in Ethiopia has been going on so long, all the food reserves have been used up. Hundreds of thousands of people are starving to death—especially children and old people. They gather together in settlement camps throughout the country. They are waiting for food to be brought in from other nations. Most of the workers at the camps know that the food cannot come fast enough, however. Many thousands more will starve before enough food can be distributed.

A Natural Disaster

What are the reasons for the failing crops and the dying livestock? Why are people starving in Ethiopia and other parts of Africa? The cause of these problems is something called drought.

As our world moves closer to the 21st century, we are becoming used to hearing about dangers to our environment. Many of these dangers are things people are responsible for, such as acid rain, pollution, and toxic waste. However, it is important to know that there are some very frightening dangers that people

Cows and other farm animals need a lot of grass and water. When a drought hits, many of these animals perish.

do not cause. Drought is one of these. It is what scientists call a natural disaster.

Simply speaking, drought is the absence of rain or other precipitation. It occurs when an area goes for a long time without getting the rain or snow it usually gets. Of course, every place on earth has its own "normal" rain level, which is enough to support the plants and wildlife that exist there. What is ample rainfall in one area might be too little or too much in another area.

For example, a tropical area might receive 100 or more inches of rain every year. The plants and animals in the tropics need that much moisture to survive. If the area's rainfall were cut in half—say, to 50 inches—that could cause a drought condition.

On the other hand, an Iowa farmer such as Chester Johnson counts on between 25 and 30 inches of rain each year. For the crops he grows and the livestock he raises, that is a perfect amount of rain. During the 1988 drought, however, Iowa received almost no rainfall. Winter snows usually supply some moisture when they melt in the spring, but snow, too, was rare in 1988.

More Than Just a Lack of Rain

Drought is more than just a lack of rain, and its effects are felt not only by farmers. Through the centuries, drought and its effects have caused the deaths of hundreds of millions of people. Untold numbers of animals have perished, too.

What do people know about this natural disaster? What kinds of damage do droughts cause, and how do people prepare for them? Is there any way to fight the effects of drought in the world?

DROUGHTS IN HISTORY

Droughts have been occurring throughout history, in almost every part of the world. Although droughts are caused by nature, people have sometimes added to the problem.

Droughts in Ancient Times

Droughts are mentioned in the Bible. The Old Testament tells the story of a young man named Joseph. He predicted that Egypt would have seven good years of farming followed by seven years of drought. The ruler of Egypt at the time believed Joseph's prediction. He ordered people in his kingdom to be careful with the food they grew. He told them to use their food wisely and put extra away. This extra, or surplus, collected over seven years, would see them through the seven years of drought. Joseph's words came true, and because of their careful planning, the people of Egypt survived the drought.

The stories of the Old Testament were written down a long time after they happened. The first eyewitness account historians have of a drought was found on an Egyptian ruler's tomb. The writing tells of a drought that struck Egypt more than five thousand years ago.

The ancient Egyptian farmers depended on the Nile River to irrigate their crops. In the summer, heavy rains made the Nile overflow its banks. The extra water provided moisture for the thirsty plants. But in this particular period, the heavy summer rains did not come. According to the writing on the tomb, none of Egypt's crops grew, and many people starved to death.

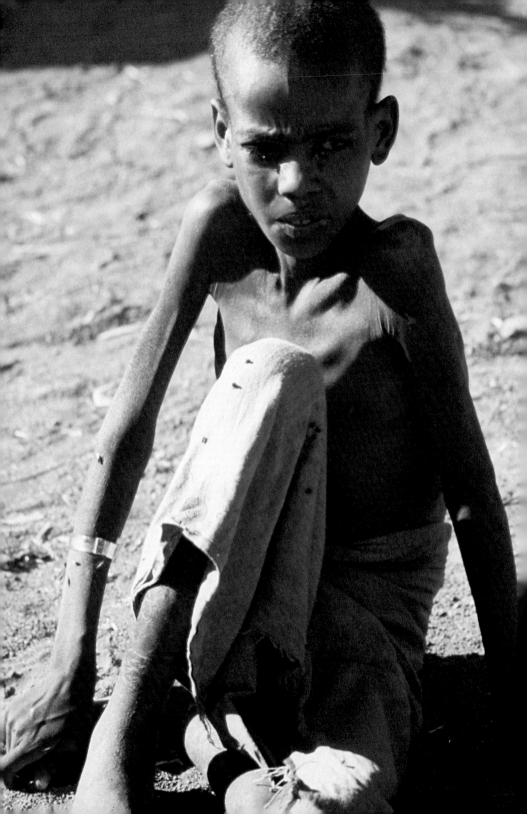

Killer Droughts in Asia

For three years beginning in 1767, a deadly drought occurred in India. In an area just east of modern India, in what is known now as Bangladesh, the rains stopped. A land that, even during good weather, was struggling to survive was almost destroyed. More than ten million people—one-third of the population of Bangladesh—died because of the drought.

Many of these people starved to death. But some died as a result of disease. When people are weak from not eating, their bodies cannot fight off even common illnesses such as colds or sore throats.

Another major drought occurred in China. This one lasted three years, too. Between 1876 and 1879, lack of rain caused the largest area of farmland in northern China to dry up. Millions of people were left without food.

China is very large, and there were other parts of the country that wanted to help. Food was collected in the large city of Tianjin, in eastern China. The plan was to send large wagonloads of grain and other supplies to the starving people.

However, most of the food never even reached its destination. China's roads were poor, and the traveling was difficult. Along the way, many of the wagons were attacked by hungry people. They were not interested in grain; they wanted to eat the camels and oxen that were being used to pull the wagons!

Those wagons that were not attacked by hungry mobs of people had trouble, too. As they got closer and closer to the starving villages, the roads were completely blocked. Thousands of dead bodies littered the roads. These were people who had been trying to escape to find food somewhere else. The wagons could not get through.

Droughts have caused famines in countries around the world.   11

Hunger made people desperate for even a mouthful of food. Historians tell us that many families sold their children for a bowl of rice or a loaf of bread. The children would be used as slaves and (the parents hoped) would be fed by their masters.

This drought in China is thought to have caused more deaths than any drought recorded in history. Approximately 13 million people died as a result of this drought! That is more than the death toll for World War II!

Five Million Killed in the U.S.S.R.

Drought was also responsible for many of the five million who died in the Soviet Union in 1921. This drought killed all of the crops in the Volga River Valley, leaving more than 30 million people without food. The Soviet Union was already short on food. The Russian Revolution in 1917 and World War I had left the large nation low on grain and other food supplies.

The drought in 1921 made a bad situation even worse. Relief agencies around the world tried to help, but they had trouble getting the food to the rural areas where the starving people were. Poor farmers and their families were so hungry that they were making bread out of baked dirt, water, bark, and acorns.

THE DIRTY THIRTIES

The United States has suffered from killer droughts, too. In the 1930s, a period of low rainfall turned the middle of the United

Dust storms like this one were common in the Great Plains states during the 1930s.

States into a baked desert. Because the scorching winds were filled with dirt and dust from the baking farmlands, this time in U.S. history is often called the "Dirty Thirties."

The drought of the 1930s was an example of a natural disaster made worse by people's ignorance. Scientists and historians say that even if a drought like the one in the thirties should happen again, there would not be as much destruction. We know now how to stop much soil loss. We just have to put that knowledge into practice.

The Mistakes of the Thirties

The root of the problem began with the large groups of settlers coming to the Great Plains states—Nebraska, Kansas, Colorado, Texas, and Oklahoma. In the late 19th century, people from the eastern part of the United States were heading west. The nation was opening up; there was new opportunity for people who wanted to leave the crowded areas of the East. Land was cheap, and the stories of rich soil, crystal-clear lakes, and abundant game tempted many.

Most of the newcomers were interested in farming or ranching. They purchased huge sections of land and staked their claims. The ranchers allowed their sheep and cattle to graze on the lush prairie grasses. The farmers got to work digging up the prairie, clearing away the grasses to get to the rich soil. They wanted to get their crops of wheat and corn planted as soon as possible.

Modern farmers know that these early ranchers and farmers made big mistakes in how they used the land. The Great Plains were covered by a thick, coarse mat of grass. Although the farmers didn't realize it then, this grass was extremely important. The grass sent down hundreds of tiny roots. These roots acted like a

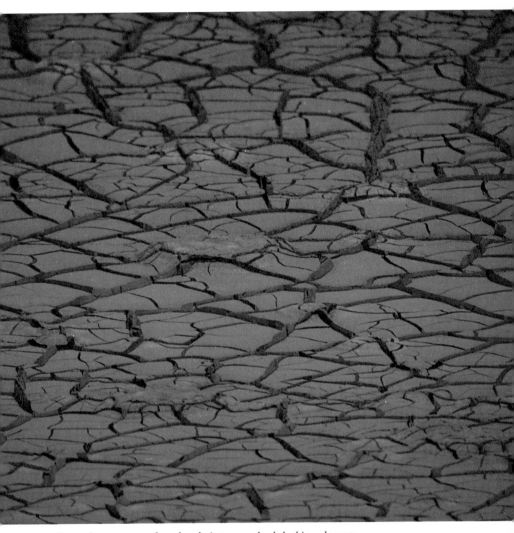

Droughts can turn farmlands into parched, baking deserts.

kind of glue, holding down the rich topsoil so that it could not blow away.

The ranchers didn't understand that when their herds of sheep and cattle ate all the grass in one area, they had to replant more grass. Instead, the ranchers simply moved their livestock to another area, then another, and then another. The farmers continued to plant more and more crops, digging up the prairie. Their crops did not hold the soil down as well as the coarse prairie grasses.

The problems got even larger during World War I. America needed lots of food to send to soldiers overseas. The farmers of the Great Plains were counted on to grow even more than before.

After the war, they were asked to increase their production even more. Many nations of Europe needed food. The war had taken place there, and farmers had been too busy fighting to plant crops. Again, the farmers of the Great Plains had to use more land to grow more food. As long as enough rain fell, the farmers and ranchers were able to grow as much as they wished.

The Dust Bowl

Drought struck in 1930, however, and again in 1932. In 1931, there was some rain, but during the next several years, almost every state in the nation experienced a shortage of rain.

For the farmers and ranchers, the drought was a nightmare. Crops, bushes, trees, and grass turned brown and died. Rivers and streams dried up. Fish and frogs died, as well as birds and other animals that depended on them for food.

One farmer remembers the drought of the 1930s as a time when nearly everyone looked at the sky. "Every morning we'd look west, wondering if any rainmakers [clouds] were rolling in.

16   *When farmers let their livestock overfeed in an area, the grasses that hold down the topsoil are destroyed. Wind turns the soil into dust storms.*

Once in a while it'd look like a storm, but by noon, the clouds had disappeared. The days were scorching hot—seemed like 100 or more every day in the summer. The only thing on anyone's mind was clouds and rain. But the sky stayed clear."

The hot, dry weather was accompanied by high winds. They blew very hard over the Great Plains, because there were no mountains or trees to hold them back. The winds whipped up the dirt, for there was no prairie grass to keep the soil down. Dry, dusty dirt was everywhere, and soon this area of the United States became known as the Dust Bowl.

The dirty wind beat against the farms and houses. Even though it was hot, people kept their doors and windows shut. But the dust came in anyway.

"I was ten years old in 1931," remembers Art LeFevere, a Kansas farmer. "I think about that dust a lot. It was on everything—the pillows, the dishes, the furniture. My mother would wipe down the table ten or twelve times every day, but you could still write your name on it with your finger, the dust was so bad.

"There were lots of days we couldn't go outside at all. The dust would go up your nose and down your throat. You'd choke to death. The only thing to do was stay inside and keep poking rags in the windows—every little crack the dust could come in."

Livestock perished from the blowing dirt. It filled their nostrils and suffocated them. People died from the dust, too. Although many wore masks over their mouths and noses, the dust still got into their lungs. Many people died from bad coughs, asthma, and pneumonia caused by the blowing dirt.

Black Blizzards

Sometimes prairie storms made the blowing dust even deadlier. The approaching storm looked like a black wall several thousand feet high. Birds and insects would fly in front of the storm, confused by the darkness.

One farmer remembers that although there were no rain clouds, there was constant thunder and lightning. The lightning was caused by the billions of dust particles, which gave off static electricity. Streaks of this "dust lightning" swirled around anything made of metal: radio antennas, cars, and gas pumps.

The dust storms of the 1930s were called "black blizzards." They made the sky so dark that people kept their lights on even during the day. The storms carried dirt from the Great Plains miles away. The dirt mixed with precipitation and was washed down out of the sky. Rain colored brown with Texas dirt fell in Wisconsin and Illinois. Snow blackened by Kansas dirt fell in Vermont. Some of the dust particles were carried high in the clouds until they fell on ships in the Atlantic Ocean!

Grasshoppers

Although most animals suffer during times of drought, one species of insect thrives. The hot, dry weather is perfect for grasshoppers.

Grasshoppers are a problem to farmers, for they eat the leaves from sprouting plants. During the 1930s, the grasshopper population was out of control. During the drought, the damage they did was not obvious. After all, few of the farmers' crops grew at all.

After rain began falling in 1936, however, it was plain to see that the population of grasshoppers had ballooned. Swarms of the

insects ate their way through groves of trees and fields of wheat, leaving nothing behind. Historians say that between 1934 and 1938, grasshoppers did more than $300 million worth of damage to crops.

A Painful Lesson

Scientists say that the drought and dust storms were made worse by people's lack of knowledge. Farmers and ranchers need to be careful with the soil. Once the fertile topsoil is blown away, crops cannot grow.

Droughts have struck the Great Plains area since the 1930s. However, none have done as much damage as the drought of the 1930s. A painful lesson has been learned. Widespread damage, such as that of the Dirty Thirties, where 50 million acres of farmland were ruined, should not happen again.

THE WATER CYCLE

There are hundreds of rainstorms going on throughout the world every moment. Somewhere, raindrops are falling and helping plants grow. Occasionally, however, the rains do not come, and there is a drought.

Why are there droughts? Why do the rains fall some years and not others? To answer these questions, it helps to understand how rain is formed in the first place.

Grasshoppers are one of the few insects that thrive during a drought. When rain begins to fall again, these creatures devour almost every plant in sight.

One Trillion Tons of Rain

Scientists know that the amount of water on earth and in the atmosphere around earth stays the same. No new water is ever formed; no water is ever lost. The water may change form: It may freeze into ice, or it may evaporate into air. However, there is no more or less water today than there was thousands of years ago.

The water in your city swimming pool once may have been drunk by Abraham Lincoln. Today's rain once may have been bathwater for an ancient Roman! This constant use and reuse of water is called the water cycle.

Every day one trillion (that's 1,000,000,000,000) tons of precipitation fall on the earth. Some of that water comes down as rain, some as snow or hail. Much of it falls into the oceans. Most of the rain that falls on the land soaks into the ground. It winds up being stored by nature, deep under the ground.

The same amount of water is evaporated by the sun every day. The sun's heat changes water from oceans, lakes, rivers, and even puddles, into moist air. That air rises high into the sky, forming clouds.

Occasionally the clouds get so heavy and swollen from the moisture inside them that they drop rain or snow. The precipitation falls on the earth. The sun dries up the moisture, and the whole process starts all over again.

We know from the water cycle that rain and snow are falling in the same amounts they always have. However, the rain does not always fall in the same place. An area that usually gets 30 inches of rain each year might sometimes get 60 or 20. The water cycle only shows us that the rain is falling. However, there seems to be no guarantee that the rain will fall in the same amounts in the same place year after year.

This rain forest is a perfect example of the water cycle. Each day water evaporates from the plants and returns to the atmosphere to fall back again as rain.

What are the reasons weather changes in a place from year to year?

Putting Together the Puzzle

A climatologist is a scientist who studies weather. Climatologists are interested in finding out if weather has changed or stayed the same over the years. By learning about the world's weather over many centuries, they can try to piece together an explanation of why droughts (or any other natural disasters) occur.

Climatologists do a special kind of detective work. Although there has always been weather on earth, people have not been keeping records of it for very long. Most of the weather records used by scientists go back only to 1890. A century is not much time to give a clear picture of weather patterns. This is where the detective work comes in.

Scientists have looked through old documents, letters, diaries—anything that might mention the weather. Newspapers dating back hundreds of years sometimes tell about the weather. Often old financial reports mention whether the year brought a good harvest. A good harvest would mean, of course, that no drought had occurred.

Some climatologists have found ways to learn about the weather for the last seven hundred years. They do this by studying tree rings. For each year a tree lives, it puts another layer, or ring, on its truck.

When a tree is cut down, people can see these rings. Scientists have found that the rings are often different thicknesses. The wider the ring, the better the tree grew that year. A thin ring indicates that there was very little rain and the tree did not grow much at all.

24   *A climatologist is a scientist who studies weather. This man is checking the rainfall for a certain area.*

Since many kinds of trees live to be several hundreds of years old, it is possible for scientists to see the weather patterns for many centuries. One climatologist found a tree that had rings going back to the year 1200! This tree showed that there had been several very severe droughts between 1200 and 1400, one lasting 38 years.

These scientific studies seem to indicate that droughts do have a pattern. Droughts in the United States seem to happen about every 22 years. The same pattern seems true for the nations of Africa. In China, drought occurs more frequently—once every ten years.

WHY DO DROUGHTS OCCUR?

Scientists have many ideas why droughts occur. There is a lot of scientific evidence to support some of these ideas. Others are not so easy to prove.

One common notion about the cause of droughts has to do with monsoons. Monsoons are powerful sea winds that blow onto land in Southeast Asia. These winds pick up moisture from the Indian Ocean and drop the moisture down as rain. The nations of Southeast Asia depend on these rainstorms to help their crops grow.

Sometimes, during the monsoon season, a strong west wind blows. This wind carries rain clouds out to sea. The rain falls on the ocean instead of on land. In cases such as this, a drought occurs in Southeast Asia.

A rain forest in Southeast Asia. Farmers there rely on the monsoon rains to water their crops.

Another cause of droughts has to do with the temperature of the land. Climatologists know that heat is an important part of the water cycle. If the sun cannot warm the water, it cannot pick up moisture from the oceans.

Several things can interfere with the sun's heating ability. Sometimes air pollution is very heavy. The chemicals in the air prevent the sun's heat from reaching the ground. Volcanos, too, send particles into the air. These may block the heat of the sun. Scientists have found that in places that have active volcanos, droughts occur when volcanic ash is blown into the air.

Some droughts in the United States have occurred because of a change in the prevailing winds. There is a constant current of wind, called the jet stream, which blows in a winding path from west to east. It is the jet stream, for instance, that brings rain-heavy clouds from the Pacific Ocean all the way to the midwestern part of the United States.

Sometimes the jet stream changes its path a little bit. It still follows a west-to-east pattern, but it may be pushed to the north. No one yet knows why this happens. However, climatologists can tell when the jet stream changes. Rainstorms and other weather conditions that seem to be heading toward Iowa or Minnesota get pushed up into Canada. When this happens consistently, a drought can occur in the areas the jet stream is avoiding.

The sun may have an effect on the jet stream. Or perhaps, as some scientists have suggested, the jet stream is affected by changes in the magnetic field that surrounds the earth.

A final theory about drought has to do with sunspots. If you have ever seen a photograph of the surface of the sun, you might have seen sunspots. They appear as little dark red areas on the sun. Actually, they are storms taking place on the sun.

Scientists have taken special pictures of the sun's surface. They have discovered that the number of sunspots changes each year. There may be a year with more than one hundred sunspots, or fifty, or none at all. Many of the droughts on earth have occurred during years in which there were fewer sunspots. Perhaps the sunspots take away some of the sun's energy, so that the earth is cooler. Again, no one knows for certain. But scientists are paying close attention to the sun's activity.

THE EFFECTS OF DROUGHT

Some people mistakenly believe that drought is a farm issue. After all, the only ones who really need to be concerned with rain are people who grow things.

This is not so. Drought is something that affects animals and plants. It affects the land and how land can be used. Drought also has drastic effects on the economy and the social life of cities and towns. It affects people's food supplies. Drought has even been a political issue, responsible for who controls the power of a nation!

Drought and the Economy

Farmers have a very risky occupation. They carefully plan what and how much they must plant. They need to worry about tools, fertilizer, and keeping on schedule with their work. However, they cannot control the weather. The rain, the heat, the wind—all of these things are "ifs" that make a difference between a farmer making money or going out of business.

An empty rain gauge is a painful sign of the damage a drought can do.

In the United States, farmers are increasingly nervous about losing money. Most are in debt; they have borrowed large sums of money to pay for seed, fertilizer, and expensive machinery. So when a drought occurs, it can mean the end to a farmer's career. Unable to sell his or her crops, the farmer cannot make money to pay back the bank loans. Most experts agree that two years of drought are enough to ruin a farmer.

When farmers go out of business, many other people are hurt as well. The banks, farm-supply dealers, and other businesses in a farming community suffer. Young people often decide to leave the farms. Their future looks bleak, for their communities are in serious financial trouble. When they leave, it makes the future of farming seem even more depressing.

Not only farmers are hurt economically. A summer without rain lowers the levels of rivers and streams. The Mississippi River dropped during the drought of 1988. The shallow water made it impossible for barges and other river traffic to move.

A winter without snow creates drought, too. In 1980, the New England states were without their usual blanket of snow. Ski lodges and resorts that depend on money from tourists had to close down. When such places do not operate, restaurants, hotels, and other businesses suffer, too.

Harm to the Environment

Droughts do a great deal of harm to the natural environment. Much of this damage is evident in the rivers and streams. In times of normal snowfall and rainfall, they are constantly replenished. But when drought strikes, the rivers, streams, and lakes become shallower.

Animals (including people) that depend on this water suffer. Fish and frogs die by the millions. Birds and other animals that feed on the fish die of starvation.

Because the temperature during a drought is usually quite warm, the water in streams and rivers becomes stagnant. Bacteria that can be harmful grow and multiply. One deadly type of bacteria, called botulism, killed hundreds of thousands of ducks during the 1988 drought in the United States. The birds became sick from eating fish and plants in the hot, murky water. The disease spread when insects laid eggs in the dead, infected ducks. When the young insects hatched from these eggs, they, too, were infected and spread the disease to other animals that ate them.

Forest fires are also a danger when droughts occur. During seasons of normal rain, trees and ground cover contain moisture. When there is no rain, however, the slightest spark—whether from a match or a lightning strike—can set off a huge blaze.

In 1871, the town of Peshtigo, Wisconsin, perished in just such a forest fire. The area had been hit hard by a drought that summer and the previous winter. The trees and grasses were dry and brittle. And because the town was almost entirely constructed of wood, there was no place safe from the flames and smoke. Once the forests around Peshtigo were ignited, the fire spread with frightening speed. Fifteen hundred people died in that fire.

Sinkholes and Other Surprises

During one drought, a man went out in his backyard and found that a 40-foot-deep hole had swallowed up his tool shed! Scientists call this a sinkhole and say that they are common during droughts. They are about 50 feet wide and can be anywhere from 40 to 100 feet deep.

A drought can also cause forest fires. When the ground becomes dry, trees can easily catch fire, and soon whole forests can be wiped out.

Sinkholes are caused by the caving in of underground crevices. Generally, there are lots of pockets under the ground that contain water. This groundwater, as it is called, feeds streams and rivers.

During times of drought, the groundwater supply gets used up. The pockets that were full of water gradually become empty. When they are empty, the soil around the pockets caves in, and the ground above them sinks. This sinking is what causes the large, deep holes that show up during times of drought.

DROUGHT AND HUMAN SUFFERING

The Dust Bowl of the 1930s was a catastrophe for the United States. All other droughts in this country are measured against it. However, it is important to understand that droughts can be far more deadly than that one. In nations that have large populations and poor farming methods, the most feared effect of drought is famine.

Famine is what happens when a nation cannot feed its people. It is mass starvation: People cannot get enough to eat, and they die. Famine occurs most often in places where the standard of living is poor. In many third-world countries, farmers have trouble growing enough food even during times of ample rainfall. During a drought, however, famine is a very real possibility.

In Africa, much of the land used for growing is poor. Even in the best years, harvests are not good. Because of this, there is no chance to put food aside. There are no surpluses to save for when droughts and famine occur.

Making a Bad Situation Worse

The farmers in America's Dust Bowl made drought worse because they did not manage the land wisely. Many of Africa's people, too, are making their droughts more serious than they need be.

Many of the farming methods in African countries increase the likelihood of drought. Good farmers know that, over the years, soil needs to be rested occasionally. Growing things on land takes out important nutrients that the soil needs. If the land is to be used over and over again, it must have these nutrients replenished. Some farmers allow a field to lie fallow, or idle, for a season. A field that is fallow can absorb nutrients from the rain and regain its growing power. This is called rotation farming. Another way of increasing the soil's growing power is by using fertilizers.

In nations such as Ethiopia, Sudan, and Kenya, however, farmers have no money for fertilizer. And they are reluctant to "waste" land by letting it lie fallow. Many families are so poor that they would starve if they did not use every available inch of growing space.

The result is dry, sandy soil with almost no growing power. The top 10 inches of dirt is called topsoil. It is becoming thinner and thinner. Because it has lost its nutrients, the soil blows away or is eroded by the wind. In many parts of Africa, 10 inches of topsoil have eroded to 2 or 3 sandy inches. Scientists also say that topsoil is hard to replace. Nature takes about one hundred years to create each inch!

Another factor that makes drought worse is political unrest in a country. Sometimes during times of civil war, food can be used as a weapon. In Ethiopia, one band of rebels blew up several trucks carrying 500 tons of grain. The grain was on its way to a settlement camp where thousands of starving people were waiting. The rebels told reporters that their war was more important than food. According to them, controlling who starved and who was fed gave the rebels an advantage in their war.

In many poor nations, efforts to help the victims of famine are in vain. Poor roads and a limited supply of vehicles make it difficult to get the food to the people who need it.

Sometimes, too, a drought-stricken nation may be reluctant to admit that it needs help. The emperor of Ethiopia once refused to tell any outside country that his nation was in the midst of a drought. He was worried that tourists would not come to Ethiopia. As a result, he said, the country would lose money. Some rulers also worry that by admitting that their people are starving their governments might seem weak.

CAN ANYTHING BE DONE?

As long as there have been farmers, there have been people anxious for rain. Native Americans had sacred dances meant to bring rain. They believed that by honoring their gods they would bring good growing weather to their corn crops.

Early American settlers, too, had ideas about how to bring rain. It was not unusual during droughts for farmers to hire a rainmaking expert. These so-called experts were often confidence

Fertilizer can restore nutrients to the soil. This farmer in China carries fertilizer in buckets.

(or "con") men. They traveled through the countryside with a collection of chemicals and gadgets.

After being paid a fee, the expert would release special gases or chemicals into the air. He promised farmers that they would see results in several hours. That was usually enough time for the rain-maker to collect his belongings and get out of town!

C. W. Post, who later became famous for his breakfast cereal company, once tried a new rainmaking scheme. He thought that heavy explosions might cause rain. He paid his workers to set off powerful dynamite charges into the air. According to his plan, the dynamite would make smoke clouds and the loud noise would shake rain from the clouds!

Seeding Clouds

Scientists have designed one method of making rain that does work sometimes. It is called cloud-seeding, and it has become very controversial.

The idea behind cloud-seeding is that clouds need to become heavy if they are to drop their moisture as rain. Many clouds have some moisture in them, but are not heavy enough. Cloud-seeding is the planting of particles of a chemical called silver iodide in clouds. The silver iodide mixes with the moisture in the cloud and makes it heavier.

Cloud-seeding is done by pilots flying in specially equipped planes. Experts say that timing is very important. Clouds form and break up in less than one hour. Seeding has to be done as soon as a likely looking cloud appears. Now, the Soviets send missiles from the ground to break up clouds.

The controversy has arisen because some farmers think that cloud-seeding is unfair. By seeding a cloud in Nebraska, and by

With irrigation, large portions of desert have been turned into valuable farmland.

making that cloud rain on farms in that state, other states are being deprived of rain. The same cloud formation might have dumped its rain later in Kansas, for instance. When the rain is tampered with, some people will get the moisture they need while others will not.

Cloud-seeding is not guaranteed to work, either. The process works only sometimes and only on the right type of cloud. Besides, say scientists, that certain type of cloud does not come along too often during a real drought, anyway.

Tapping Other Sources of Water

Rain is not the only way crops can be watered. Irrigation is another way. Irrigation is using water from a river to water crops. River water is halted from its natural path by large dams. The water is moved aside into reservoirs, or holding areas.

When water is needed in a particular place, workers at the dam can let a little water through. It travels through special irrigation ditches that have been cut into the soil. Irrigation is much like creating your own series of rivers!

The city of Los Angeles relies on irrigation for its water supply. The city is actually in a desert, but one would never guess it because of the green grass and beautiful gardens. Water for Los Angeles comes from the Colorado River, 230 miles to the north. With a series of dams and irrigation pipes, the river water is diverted to southern California. There it is used for drinking and growing crops.

Groundwater is another source of water. Farmers know that they can tap the deep underground reserves of water and have a big supply. In fact, there is 30 times more fresh water underground than in all the rivers and lakes in the United States! This seems like

Irrigation ditches bring water into desert areas from dams far away.

a lot of water, and it is. But there is not enough water to allow everyone to irrigate. When one city or one farm uses a lot of water, others can't use it. They are left without water.

Groundwater reserves are anywhere from 100 to 600 feet down, and drilling is expensive. After the water supply is tapped, it must be brought to the surface and sprayed on the fields. More than 100 gallons of groundwater per minute can be sprayed onto the farmer's fields. This equipment, too, is very expensive. A single sprayer costs about $100,000!

Some farmers call this type of farming "rain renting." There are advantages, of course, since farmers no longer have to worry as much about hot, dry weather withering their crops. However, many farmers feel that rain renting is too expensive. They feel that rain renters have traded one set of problems for another.

A Global Problem

Drought and its effects are global problems. That means that all the nations of the world are affected. It also means that we are all responsible for finding ways to help.

When drought struck in Ethiopia, many nations of the world helped by sending aid. The same happened in India and again in Kenya. But sending money and food are only partial solutions. Experts say that the most helpful assistance would be to teach better farming methods to the people of these nations.

Zimbabwe is an example of a nation that has learned to fight drought. In 1985, it was hit hard by drought, and hundreds of thousands of people were starving. However, the farmers there learned to be more careful with the land.

Volunteers from the United States and other nations showed the Zimbabwe farmers how important it was to plant trees. The

42   *When a drought occurred in Ethiopia, relief organizations from around the world sent emergency food and medical supplies.*

trees would act as a break against the wind and would anchor the topsoil. The Zimbabwe farmers also learned how to create irrigation systems. Today, they not only grow enough food to feed themselves, but they also export food to other countries.

Scientists around the world are working to create new kinds of seeds. These new seeds will be hardier and better suited to dry weather. They will also grow more quickly, in twelve weeks as opposed to nine months.

People will probably never be able to control weather. There will always be periods of drought. But farming methods can be improved. Large stockpiles of extra food can be stored for times when famine strikes. By working together, the nations of the world can fight the deadly effects of drought.

FOR MORE INFORMATION

Food First
1885 Mission Street
San Francisco, CA 94103

Land Stewardship Project
14758 Ostland Trail North
Marine, MN 55047
(612) 433-2770

FOR FURTHER READING

Blumberg, Rhoda. *Famine.* New York: Franklin Watts, 1978.

Fradin, Dennis Brindell. *Disaster! Droughts.* Chicago: Children's Press, 1983.

Gardner, Robert. *Water.* New York: Julian Messner, 1982.

Johnson, Thomas P. *When Nature Runs Wild.* Mankato, MN: Creative Education Press, 1968.

National Geographic Society. *Powers of Nature.* Washington, DC: National Geographic Society, 1978.

Timberlake, Lloyd. *Famine in Africa.* New York: Gloucester Press, 1986.

GLOSSARY

botulism *Deadly bacteria that appear in stagnant, warm water.*

climatologist *A scientist who studies weather patterns.*

cloud-seeding *A way of making a cloud heavier so that the moisture within it will come down as rain.*

Dirty Thirties *A time of drought in the United States during the 1930s.*

drought *An extended time without normal amounts of rainfall.*

Dust Bowl *Refers to the Great Plains states during the drought of the 1930s in America. These states were troubled by strong, hot winds that blew much of the growing soil away.*

erosion *The wearing away of topsoil by strong winds.*

fallow *Idle, unused.*

famine *An extreme shortage of food that can cause mass starvation.*

groundwater *A supply of water found underground.*

irrigation *The channeling of water from rivers to farmers' fields or city holding tanks.*

jet stream *Strong winds blowing across the United States. The jet stream blows from west to east.*

monsoons *Strong winds that periodically bring storms and rain to Southeast Asia.*

natural disaster *A calamity caused not by people, but by nature. Tornados, floods, and droughts are natural disasters.*

reservoir *A holding area for water to be used for irrigation.*

sinkhole *A caving in of dirt around an underground pocket.*

sunspots *Storms occurring on the surface of the sun.*

surplus *The extra food that remains after people use what they need.*

topsoil *The fertile, rich soil in which crops may grow.*

water cycle *The process by which water is used over and over in nature.*

INDEX